HOPELESS HEROES

★ *JASON'S*
WILD
WINDS!

STELLA
TARAKSON

Sweet
Cherry

Published by Sweet Cherry Publishing Limited
Unit 36, Vulcan House,
Vulcan Road,
Leicester, LE5 3EF
United Kingdom

First published in the UK in 2020
2020 edition

2 4 6 8 10 9 7 5 3 1

ISBN: 978-1-78226-350-0

© Stella Tarakson

Hopeless Heroes: Jason's Wild Winds

Cover design by Nick Roberts and Amy Booth
Illustrations by Nick Roberts

www.sweetcherrypublishing.com

Printed and bound in China
C.WM004

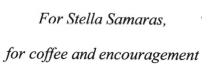
For Stella Samaras,

for coffee and encouragement

1

'Oh no, not again!' Tim Baker watched his
model raft slide under the water's surface
and hit the bottom of the bathtub. He

dunked a hand into the water and fished the dripping raft out, glaring at it. That was the tenth time it had sunk. He'd tried everything: changing the length of the twigs, the width of the twigs, how he tied them together, and the type of string he used. Nothing worked. No matter what he did, the stupid thing kept sinking. The last thing Tim needed was another F at school.

Frowning, he sank onto his knees beside the tub. It might've helped if Leo had bothered to turn up! They were meant to be doing the project together. Not that they wanted to be paired up – Miss Omiros had forced them to work together. It was now late Sunday afternoon. The

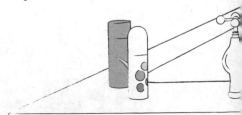

project was due tomorrow, and Tim had been struggling on his own all weekend. The bully expected Tim to do all the work, but would still take a share of the glory.

TYPICAL!

Except ... it was becoming clear that there'd be no glory. The raft kept sinking and Tim was out of ideas on how to fix it.

Pain flared in his jaw and Tim grimaced. The toothache that had started as a mild twinge a few days ago

was becoming stronger. More frequent, too. He knew he should tell Mum, but she would insist on a visit to the dentist. Enough said.

Tim glowered at the raft as if it were to blame. Putting it on the floor, he resisted the urge to kick it. Just then, the doorbell rang. He heard Mum open the front door and call out, 'Tim, your friend's here!'

Did she mean Ajay? Feeling cheered, Tim ran down the stairs. Knowing him, Ajay's raft would be finished already. Maybe he could give Tim a few pointers. But the sight that greeted Tim through the doorway stopped him in his tracks.

On the doorstep stood Leo and an angry-looking old woman. Tim

recognised her as the bully's grandmother.
Her grey hair was pulled back in a
bun that was as severe as her scowl.
Her wrinkled hands clutched at Leo's
shoulders like an
eagle's talons.

'Now get in
there and do your
project,' the woman
growled, pushing
him over the
threshold. 'Don't
come home before
it's done – or I'll fix
you up!'

'Yes, Nan,' Leo
said, his head

bowed. The boy's face was red and he kept his gaze on the floor as he clomped up the stairs and followed Tim into the bathroom.

Embarrassed, Tim said nothing. He could see the look of misery on Leo's face. His eyes were watery and red-rimmed. Had he been crying? It didn't seem possible, not given how tough Leo always acted. And what was that phrase his nan had used? "Fix you up"? That's what Leo kept threatening to do to Tim!

'Um,' Tim said eventually, needing to break the awkward silence. He dragged his gaze away from the boy's face. 'I haven't had much luck with the raft. It keeps sinking.'

Leo shrugged his beefy shoulders.
'Whaddya expect me to do about it?'

'Do you know how to fix it?' Tim
decided to ignore the aggression in Leo's
voice.

'Why would I?'

'I just thought you might have an idea.
I asked my mum but she didn't know.' Tim
could have asked Mum's boyfriend Larry
who was a teacher at their school, but
he wanted to show him that he could do
things on his own. 'Hey, how about your
parents? Would your mum or dad know
what to do?'

Leo's answer was abrupt.

'Have you asked them?'

The boy clenched his fists. 'No.'

'Why not?' Tim persisted. 'It wouldn't hurt to ask, would it? Maybe you can ring them up–'

'I don't have parents,' Leo said through gritted teeth. 'Happy now?'

'Sorry,' Tim mumbled, feeling his own cheeks turn red. He didn't want to ask any more questions, but he was beginning to realise that Leo's home life wasn't awfully happy. He might even understand him a little bit better now. Tim's own father had died when he was little, but Tim's mother had never let him feel unloved. He was also grateful for his friendship with the hero Hercules. Although the demigod lived in Ancient Greece, Tim could go and see him whenever he liked.

Tim had first met Hercules when he accidentally broke an old Greek vase that the hero had been trapped in. By repairing the vase and solving the riddle on it, Tim was able to send the hero back home. Since then, Tim had been using the vase to travel to and from Ancient Greece. There he'd befriended Hercules' daughter Zoe, and together they'd had many adventures,

encountering dangerous creatures and trying to escape the wicked goddess Hera.

Tim had also met many interesting – if somewhat bizarre – people. People like Theseus the vain heart-throb, Perseus the flower fanatic, and Jason the boat builder.

Tim started.

JASON!

Why hadn't he thought of him before? Jason could help fix the raft, no problem at all! The last time Tim had seen the distracted hero, he'd been building a boat to replace the *Argo*, the ship he'd sailed on to retrieve the Golden Fleece. A model raft would be nothing to him!

'I've got an idea.' Tim scooped up the raft and looked at Leo. 'Stay here, I'll be right back,' he said, as he ran out of the room.

Tim dashed into his bedroom where he kept
the magic vase. He opened the wardrobe
door and whipped off the sheet covering the
large Greek amphora. Knowing it would
bring him back before Leo even noticed he
was gone, Tim grabbed the big black handles.

'Oh vase,' he said, 'take me to Jason and
the *Argonut*'

Tim held on tight as the vase took
him soaring through time and space, the

now-familiar golden mist
glittering around his body.
He hoped the vase would take him
to a time when Jason had finished building
his new boat, the *Argonut*. Otherwise he'd
be too busy with his own work to have
time for Tim's raft.

Tim expected to land at Jason's home,
where they'd met before. Tim and Zoe
had been searching for the Golden Fleece,
only to have Jason tell them he'd given it
to his girlfriend Arachne. Unknown to the
boat-obsessed Jason, Arachne had been
turned into a giant spider, who had woven
the fleece into a pair of gloves. Luckily it
had kept its magical healing properties,
and the children were able to rescue the

people who'd been turned to stone by Medusa, the snake-haired gorgon. Since then, Tim had vowed to always keep the gloves with him in case he ever needed them again ... but most of the time he forgot. Like now.

He made a mental note to remember them next time, but it promptly fled his mind when he touched solid ground. This was not Jason's house! The vase had brought Tim to a place he'd never been before. Grappling with the raft and the unwieldy vase, Tim gazed at his surroundings.

He was standing at the edge of a vast, glittering ocean. A fresh, salty smell filled the air and a light wind whipped around

his face. A few metres away, at the end
of an old wharf, stood a shiny new boat.
A young man was waxing it lovingly. He
had closely-shaven hair with a long tuft
on top. He was so concentrated on his

work that he didn't look around when Tim approached.

'Jason?' Tim tried to get his attention. 'We've met before, remember? I'm Tim Baker.'

Jason grunted but otherwise ignored him.

'My friend and I were looking for the fleece,' Tim tried again. 'And you told us–'

'Hold this, will ya?' Without turning his head, Jason thrust a cloth at Tim.

'Um, sure.' Tim put the vase down so he could grab the cloth. 'As I was saying–'

'How do you like my new ride?' Jason spoke over him. 'Isn't she awesome?'

'Err ...' Suddenly, Tim remembered. The only way to get Jason's attention was to imitate the way he talked and – more importantly – praise his boat. 'None finer, bro,' Tim said. He was kind of relieved that Zoe wasn't there to laugh at him.

'For real? Cool.' Jason finally looked at him. 'I know you, don't I? Hey, yeah. You're the little bro who was asking me about her buoyancy.' Jason patted the boat as it bobbed up and down in the water. 'The only way to know for sure is to test her out, which I'm just about to do. I've been looking forward to this moment forever, ya know?'

'I hear ya.' Tim nodded solemnly.

The sail caught a gust of air and billowed, as if the boat itself were growing impatient.

'She's all set up and raring to go. Much as I'd love to hang around and chat, I can't wait anymore.' Jason turned and cast an eager glance at the boarding plank. 'Catch ya later.'

'NO! WAIT!'

Tim's voice was more shrill than he intended.

'You wanna come along?' Jason asked, looking over his shoulder at Tim. 'I don't mind, long as you're quick.'

'No. Well, yes.' It would be fun, come to think of it. But Tim didn't want to forget the purpose of his visit. 'I wanted to ask you a favour first. Can you please fix my raft?'

But Jason already had one foot on the plank. 'What, you mean now? Don't think so, bro.'

'But – but, you're so good at it,' Tim said beseechingly. 'It wouldn't take long and no one else is as good at making boats as you are. Err ... bro.'

Jason couldn't help looking pleased at the compliment. 'Oh go on then. Give it here. Long as it's quick.'

Spirits rising, Tim thrust the raft at the boat builder.

Jason hummed and hawed as he turned it over in his hands.

'Well here's your problem!' he said after a moment. 'The mast is way too long and it's totally in the wrong place.' Snorting in disbelief, he threw the raft into the sea, where it promptly plummeted to the bottom. 'Little bro, what were you thinking? Gimme my kit.'

Tim rushed to pick up the satchel that Jason was pointing at. The hero dug around and extracted offcuts of wood, cloth and pieces of string. Tim watched in awed silence as a small, sleek boat started to form in Jason's hands. His fingers moved quickly and confidently. He made a mast and sail and deftly secured the whole thing together.

'There ya go,' Jason said, holding out an exact replica of the *Argonut* and grinning.

'Wow, thank you!' Tim took the model boat reverently. 'That looks amazing. Does it float?'

'Course it does. Now are you coming for a ride or what? You can help work the sail.'

Tim was tempted. He'd never been on a boat before. And to actually go sailing with *the* Jason from Jason and the Argonauts ... it was too good an opportunity to pass up!

'I'd love to,' Tim said, quickly making up his mind. 'What do I do with my stuff?' He nodded at his vase.

'Give it here,' Jason said, and stowed the vase securely on the boat. 'And that.' He took the model out of Tim's hands and tucked it next to the vase. 'Come on, let's ride.'

Tim couldn't help thinking about Zoe, however, who had a constant yearning for adventure. 'Can my friend come too? She'd absolutely love to ...'

'You mean that bossy chick?' Jason clearly remembered their last encounter. 'She's Hercules' daughter, right?' He scratched his head contemplatively. 'Yeah, better bring her along or Herc will whinge that I upset her. But be quick or I'm going without ya!'

'I'll be quick,' Tim agreed. He turned to leave then stopped. 'Um ... which way do I go?'

■　■　■

Repeating Jason's directions to himself, Tim ran towards Zoe's house.

'Someone's in a hurry,' a figure muttered as Tim darted by.

Not slowing down, Tim turned his head and flashed an apologetic grin. It was

Hermes, the messenger god. The wings on his cap and sandals fluttered in greeting.

'Sorry-in-a-rush!' Tim panted.

'How come?' Hermes called after him.

Tim pretended that he hadn't heard. He picked up his pace. Long explanations would only delay him, and besides, he was starting to think that Zoe might be right. Maybe they shouldn't trust Hermes. Although he acted friendly, Hermes was Hera's servant, as well as being the god of thieves and liars. But this wasn't the time to worry about it. It was time to grab his friend and have some fun.

Tim found the right house and knocked on the door. It was flung open before he'd finished knocking. Standing there, wringing her hands, was Zoe's mother.

'Where is she? Where's Zoe?' Agatha asked, her voice tight with anxiety. Tim stared at her in surprise. Normally Agatha was cool, calm and in control. Unlike her husband Hercules, she was softly spoken and thoughtful. Today, however, there was a tremble in her voice. Her normally sleek hair was tumbling out of its braid and there were dark circles under her eyes.

Tim was so taken aback it took him a moment to work out what Agatha was saying. 'Y-you mean Zoe's gone missing?' he stammered, aghast. 'When? What happened?'

Agatha stared at Tim for a moment, her face beginning to crumple.

'I ... I'm sorry,' she said, guiding him over the threshold. 'Come inside. I was ... well, I was hoping she was with you.'

Tim stepped through the doorway and into the open-air courtyard. 'No, I only just arrived. I thought she'd be here.' It felt odd, not hearing his friend's footsteps dashing towards him.

'She went to the well this morning,' Agatha said, steadying herself on the doorframe. 'I usually go with her, but I had a headache and she said she'd be okay on her own ... Oh, it's all my fault!' she wailed. 'Hercules keeps saying I shouldn't let her leave the house alone. He was right!'

'I'm sure she's okay,' Tim hastened to reassure Zoe's mother. 'How long has she been gone? Maybe she's just chatting with friends.'

'She's been gone for hours! She's not at the well, I've already checked. Nobody has seen her since early this morning.' Agatha flashed Tim a panicked look.

'Has anyone put out an alert on the GGG?' If there was a problem, it might have been announced on the Greek God Grapevine, a system that let gods tell heroes that their help was needed.

'There's nothing; Hercules checked. But something's happened to her. I can feel it.'

'I'll find her,' Tim said promptly.

'Will you, Tim Baker?' Agatha clutched his arm, like a drowning woman clutching her rescuer. 'You know my daughter well, don't you? You know where she might go.'

'Sure I do.' Tim nodded. His mind racing.

'Hercules is searching for her now,' Agatha said. 'But you know him, he's out of his mind with worry.'

Tim could believe it. Zoe thought her father was overprotective, but Tim knew that he had good reason to be. The goddess Hera, whose plans had been thwarted by Tim and Zoe, was out for revenge. Not too long ago, she had trapped Zoe in a giant puzzle prison. But surely things were different now? More recently Hera had switched her focus to Tim. Frightened of the future and the unknown powers it may hold, the goddess had made it all too clear that Tim was her new target. Why would she

bother going after Zoe? Unless ...

Unless it was a lure - an attempt to drag Tim in and capture him again? He gulped. Hera knew that Tim would keep coming back to see his friends, and she knew he wouldn't hesitate to run to Zoe's rescue ...

'Where will you look?' Agatha asked.

Tim realised he might be walking into a trap, but he couldn't let that stop him. He knew where he would go. 'Don't worry about that. I'll find her as soon as I can.'

■ ■ ■

The inside of Hera's temple was cool and dark. Tim crept around as quietly as he could, so as not to alert Hera's peacocks. There was no sign of them so far and Tim wanted to keep it that way. The peacocks acted like the goddess' guard dogs. Whenever they appeared and started to squawk, Tim knew that Hera would soon follow.

He looked around the central chamber, edging his way around the giant statue of Hera. Made of gold and ivory, the haughty goddess was sitting in

a gigantic throne
and seemed to be
glaring right at him.
In one hand she held a
pomegranate. Tim shuddered.
An image of Hera hurling the fruits at
him flashed through his memory. She had
turned the pomegranates into weapons
that exploded like hand grenades. He
slowly made his way to the other side
of the room. Apart from the statue,
there was nothing else to see here. Ever
so quietly, Tim entered the small dark
chamber where people left offerings for
the goddess. It was in here that
Hera had once hidden the vase
that had trapped Hercules. He

looked through the pile of figurines and
ornate pots. Could any of these have
been used to trap Zoe? He whispered her
name, in case she could hear him.

'Zoe. Are you here?'

Silence.

Either she wasn't there, or she was unable to answer. What if she was hurt? What if he was too late?!

Tim's tooth starting to twinge again. He looked back at the offerings and forced himself to stay calm. Panicking would get him nowhere. It would help if he knew what he was looking for. Could he be staring straight at Zoe's prison without even knowing it? Stop and think, he urged himself. What might a trap look like? Hercules had been caught in a large vase with his picture painted on it. The flask that Hera had tried to catch Tim in also had a picture of him on the front. So, if Zoe were trapped, it might be in something that had her picture on it!

Tim looked at each pot in turn. They were all different shapes and sizes. Some had drawings of battles on, while others had scenes of everyday life. None of the pictures looked even remotely like Zoe. He breathed out. It didn't look like she was there. Tim didn't know whether to feel relieved or not. But as he tried to work out what to do next, he heard heavy footsteps thunder past the temple.

4

The footsteps were far too heavy to belong
to Hera. Tim walked swiftly to the temple's
entrance and peered out. It was just as he'd
suspected. Hercules was stomping around
outside. He had a thunderous look on his face.

'Zoe!' Hercules called, his head
swivelling left and right. 'Where are you?'

Tim darted out between the columns
and ran down the stairs. 'Hercules!' he
called after the retreating figure.

The hero did not slow down. He had such a big stride, Tim had to run to catch up with him. 'Tim Baker. Have you seen my daughter?'

Tim hoped his friend wasn't blaming him for the disappearance. He didn't want to be banned from visiting again. 'N-no. I just got here.' He thought he'd better make that clear.

'Agatha told me what happened, so I've come to help you find Zoe.'

'That is good of you,' Hercules said, his brow creased with worry. 'Thank you, my friend.'

'I looked in Hera's temple …' Tim began.

Hercules shook his head as he walked on. 'I tried there too. I have tried everywhere! I even attempted to lift up a mountain to check whether she was hidden underneath.'

'So where are we going?' Tim asked, still running to keep up with Hercules.

'To consult the three Grey Women. They see that which is hidden.'

Tim had never heard of the Grey Women before, but he was glad his friend seemed to have a plan. 'You mean they're good at finding things?

What are they? Private detectives or something?'

'They have an eye,' Hercules said, as if that were explanation enough.

'Just the one?' Tim said, trying to make a joke. Sure, it was a rather feeble one, but he hated seeing Hercules so upset.

'Yes, that is correct. Just one eye.'

'What?!' Tim yelped. 'Are they all half blind?' He shot a perplexed look at the hero. Wouldn't that make finding people more difficult?

'Don't be silly,' Hercules said, frowning. 'They have one eye between them.'

Tim uttered a high-pitched laugh, then

stopped when Hercules glared at him. The
hero clearly wasn't in the mood for jokes.
But – surely he didn't mean it? How could
three people share one eye? Did they pluck
it out and pass it around? The thought
alone made Tim feel queasy.

'Where do they live?' he asked.

'In a hut by the sea. Can you walk
faster?' Hercules asked. 'Or shall I carry
you?'

Tim broke into a jog to keep up.
He stopped talking and focused on his
breathing. As they headed back towards
the coast, Tim suddenly remembered
his vase was on the *Argonut*. Had Jason
left already? Tim scanned the horizon
worriedly as they drew nearer. He couldn't

see any boats on the sea. With any luck, that meant Jason was still waiting for him.

'Hey Herc!' a voice called as they neared the water's edge. It was Jason, pacing along the wharf. 'Coming for a spin with us?' To his relief, Tim saw that the *Argonut* was still tethered and bobbing up and down in the water.

'Not now!' Hercules boomed. 'We seek the Grey Women.'

'But this is my new ride, man. Isn't she a beauty?'

'Later.' Hercules said curtly.

Jason looked offended. 'Right! So I'll be off then.'

'Wait! I need to get my vase back!' Tim yelped, but Hercules showed no sign of stopping or slowing down. If Tim lagged behind, he'd lose him. 'Can you wait a bit longer?' Tim begged Jason.

'Tell you what,' Jason said. 'I'm gonna see if anyone else from my old crew wants to ride. That'll give you more time, little bro. After that, I'm off.'

'Thank you. I'll try to be quick. Hey, wait for me!' Tim had to run to catch up with Hercules.

Together they walked up a steep path that led to the top of a cliff. Hercules strode up it easily, as if on a gentle stroll, but Tim was huffing, puffing and sweating by the time they got to the top. There, perched right on the edge of the cliff, was a crooked little hut. Made of splintering wood, it looked like it was about to break apart and fall into the sea. Hercules marched up to the door and hammered on it with his fist. Not waiting for an answer, the hero pushed the flimsy door open and marched inside.

'Who is so rude they dare to intrude?' a querulous voice asked.

Tim followed Hercules into the dark interior. Sitting around a rickety old table were three very old women, all dressed in grey. They were bald except for a few wispy hairs, and their mottled skin was stretched tightly across their bony faces. Tim gasped as he noticed their empty eye sockets – gaping black holes that followed Tim and Hercules sightlessly around as they entered. Only one of the women

actually had an eye, just as Hercules had said. Bulbous and bloodshot, it glared at them. Tim thought that she was the one who'd spoken.

'It is I, Hercules! I need you to find my daughter. At once!'

'Those who shout are soon left out,' said the woman with the eye. Her toothless mouth was shrivelled and her breath smelt of rotting fish. The other two women nodded in unison.

'Listen, you hideous hags. Don't play games with me,' Hercules said, clenching his fists. 'You will give me the information I seek – or else!'

'Do not fight, let's be polite!' said a different woman.

Tim noticed that she only had one tooth, right in the centre of her lower jaw. It was large and jagged, and a dirty brown colour. As Tim watched, she picked up a piece of bread and gnawed on it happily.

'Hurry up with that tooth, I'm starving in truth,' the woman with the eye said.

'Give me the eye and I shall try.'

Did they always speak in rhyme? But the question was abruptly chased out of Tim's mind by a sight so awful he wished he was still at home with his sinking raft. The woman with the eye stuck her claw-like fingers into her eye socket and twisted. With a wet sucking sound, the eyeball popped into her shrivelled hand. She held it out towards the woman with the tooth, who grabbed it greedily and poked it into her own face. Then, with a grimace, she yanked out her tooth and handed it over.

'That is better,' the first woman said, poking it into her gaping mouth. 'Do we have any feta?'

Tim clutched at his stomach and tried not to vomit.

'Tell me where my daughter is,' Hercules roared, 'or I shall demolish your hut!'

The three Grey Women sneered at the hero. 'Threats do not work, they make us smirk,' said the one that now had the eye.

'A gift we demand, the best in the land,' said the other.

'A gift!' Hercules stamped his foot, making the hut shake alarmingly. 'Do you expect me to have time for gifts? My daughter is missing, I cannot concern myself with anything else! Use your magic eye to tell me where she is – I beg you.'

'Then bring a gift, and make it swift.'

Tim could tell that Hercules was about to lose control. He didn't think that throwing a massive tantrum would help them find Zoe, so he butted in before the hero could react. 'I will bring you a gift.'

The old women turned their empty eye sockets towards Tim. It took all his willpower to not show how freaked out he felt. 'A very important gift,' he added, supressing a shudder. 'To help fix that tooth.' He nodded at the woman who was nibbling on some cheese.

She stopped eating long enough to shriek, 'What is wrong with our tooth? Do not lie; tell the truth.'

'Well it's dirty, isn't it?' Tim said, grateful his own tooth had stopped twinging for the moment. 'Look at my teeth. See how clean they are?' He flashed them at the woman who currently had the eyeball.

'He is right, his teeth are white,' she admitted grudgingly.

'But yours is brown. Dark brown. If you don't look after it properly, it'll soon rot away. Then how will you be able to eat?'

The women lapsed into an uncomfortable silence.

'If you tell us where Zoe is,' Tim added, 'I promise to bring you a gift that will fix your problem.'

'Bring it now, we don't care how.'

Tim could feel Hercules quaking beside him. 'No. You must tell us first,' Tim said firmly, before the hero could erupt. 'I promise to bring it to you as soon as Zoe is safe.'

The Grey Women seemed to think it through. The one with the eye said,

'You've left us no choice, so now hear my voice.'

Her eyeball started to spin around sickeningly fast – up, down, left and right. Even round to the back of her head. Tim guessed that she was looking for Zoe. Finally the eye stopped spinning and the woman spoke in a sing-song voice that reminded Tim of Apollo's oracle. 'Zoe was taken against her will, off to the place that holds her still. If

you rush to Perseus' cave, you can stop it from being her grave.'

The one without an eye or

a tooth nodded grimly and spoke for the first time. 'Now go Hercules to save your daughter, but if you're not back when you ought ter' – Tim felt that rhyme was rather forced – 'we'll release a plague upon your town, and half of your people shall go down.'

'Down? Down where?' Hercules asked, glancing at the floor.

The woman with the eyeball rolled her eye. 'She means die, you twit.' And then, realising what she'd just said, she hastily added, 'so – ahem! – that is it.'

'Right, let's go,' Tim said. He looked at the Grey Women. 'Thank you.'

'To avoid the plague do not forget, bring us our gift before sunset.'

'We won't forget,' Tim promised.
Sunset. That gave them plenty of time. He
hoped.

Hercules did not walk out the door
– he ran, grabbing Tim on his way out.
Before he knew it, Tim was on the hero's
shoulders, clinging on for dear life. His
mouth snapped open and shut from
being jolted so hard, but Tim gritted his
teeth and held on tight. As they drew
near the cave, he could see the rows and
rows of flowers that Perseus tended.
Once a great hero, the old man now
enjoyed gardening above all else. Behind
the rows of flowers was a soaring cliff
face, its ragged surface dappled with
light and shadow.

'Where is this cave?' Hercules asked, setting Tim down and looking around.

Tim had no difficulty finding the cave that he and Zoe had once hidden in. He shivered as he remembered how the gorgon had followed them. The hissing of her hair snakes, the despair on the faces of her turned-to-stone victims ...

'It's here,' Tim said, rushing to the entrance. Although he knew the gorgon was dead, decapitated by the hero Theseus, Tim still felt safer inside the cave than out. 'Perseus!' he called out to the elderly hero. 'Perseus, we're looking for Zoe. Have you seen her?'

The old man didn't reply. Instead, a girl's voice called, 'Tim! Is that you? Help!'

'Zoe!' Hercules roared. Ducking his head to avoid hitting it on the pointy stalactites, the hero bustled into the cave.

'Dad! Thank the gods you're here! Get me out.' Zoe's voice was frantic but husky, as if she had been screaming.

Tim was close on Hercules' heels as they ran into the cave. When the hero suddenly stopped, Tim bumped into him.

'Zoe!' Hercules' cry was one of pure anguish.

They were in a part of the cave that
was so narrow, Tim had to peer around
Hercules in order to catch a glimpse of
Zoe. The girl was tied to a thick limestone
column by hundreds of shining threads
that criss-crossed around her trembling
body. She strained against the cords when
she saw her rescuers. But rather than
loosening, the threads dug in more tightly,
leaving angry red marks wherever they

touched her skin. Whimpering, Zoe pulled even harder.

'Stop struggling, that's making it worse!' Tim yelped. 'I'm coming.'

He crouched down and crawled over to Zoe through Hercules' widely-spaced legs. Without waiting for the hero to react, Tim started tugging at the cords. They were remarkably strong. 'Ouch,' he complained as they bit into his fingers. It was like being stung by a bee! 'What are these things?'

'How would I know?' Zoe grimaced as the threads tightened around her waist. 'I didn't get a chance to ask questions. They must have some sort of curse on them, though, because they're really tough. Like strands of iron.'

'How did you end up here?' Tim asked, trying to tease the threads apart with his fingernails, hoping that would weaken them. But his fingertips were starting to go numb, hampering his efforts.

'Hera.'

Hercules let out a bellow of rage and kicked a stalagmite, which snapped and toppled over. 'That witch! I shall tear out her spleen! I warned her to stay away from you. How did she catch you?'

'I was on my way back from the well with the jug full of water,' Zoe said, her head drooping. 'I hadn't got far when an old lady stopped me and asked for a drink. I thought she looked harmless, so I offered her the jug.'

'She was Hera in disguise,' Tim guessed.

'Yes,' Zoe said bitterly. 'I can't believe I fell for the sweet-old-lady-at-the-well trick! When I offered her the jug – which was really heavy – she picked it up as if it were a feather. She tipped all the water out, soaking my feet, then she started cackling. I thought she was bonkers.'

'She is,' Tim said.

'Then there was this flash of light and the old women turned into Hera. I tried to run away but I slipped in the puddle of water. Hera clicked her fingers and suddenly I was here, all tied up. I yelled for hours but nobody came.'

'We'll get you out, don't worry,' Tim said, running his fingers through his hair. How, he didn't know. He still hadn't managed to remove the silver threads. What he needed was a pair of wire cutters.

'Where are we, anyway?' Zoe asked, looking around. 'This place looks familiar.'

'We're in Perseus' cave, but there's no sign of him,' Tim said.

'He's probably on one of his flower-finding missions,' Zoe groaned. 'But even if he were here, I don't think he'd be much help. He'd probably try to use me as a garden stake. How are you doing with those threads?' She shifted uncomfortably.

'They won't break,' Tim said, rubbing his fingertips. 'We need a sharp knife. Hey, do you think Perseus' scythe is still here? The one Theseus used to' – he slid finger across his throat – 'slay the gorgon?'

'You're not putting that thing anywhere near me!' Zoe said, struggling harder. 'Dad, can you untie me?'

'Me, undo those little strings? Not possible. My super-strong fingers weren't made for such delicate work. But we are wasting too much time fiddling about!' Hercules bellowed in frustration. 'Stand back, Tim Baker.' He picked Tim up and put him gently aside.

'What are you –? No! Don't do that!'

Head down like a charging bull, the hero rushed at the limestone column. He

gripped it with his saucer-sized hands, just above Zoe's head. He gave one sharp tug.

CRACK!

The entire column came away in his hands, along with a sizeable chunk of the cave floor. Hercules slid Zoe off the top of the broken column, threads and all. The bindings, now lying slack on her dusty chiton, cascaded to the floor. Zoe was stunned but free. 'Thank the—' she started to say.

An ominous rumbling sound came from deep within the cave. Tim felt the ground shake beneath his feet. 'Uh oh,' he said. Breaking that column must have destabilised one of the tunnels that snaked into the mountainside. 'We'd better get out of–'

Before he could finish, the rumbling turned into a roar. A shower of dust and pebbles rained down on their heads, covering them with a thick layer of dirt. Tim clamped his hands over his nose and mouth. 'Hurry!' he said, his voice muffled, 'before the roof falls in!' He turned and started to lead the way.

Tim didn't see what happened next, but he heard and felt it. A loud, ground-shaking thud, followed by a high-pitched scream and a furious bellow.

He whipped
around. A boulder
must have slid
out of place and
toppled over. It
had landed on
Zoe, pinning her
to the ground.
The girl's
face was
pale and
screwed
up in
pain.

'Zoe! Do not fear, I will release you.'

'That is better! Am I not an excellent
father?' Hercules' chest jutted out with

pride. 'Let us go home, your mother is worried.'

Zoe didn't reply, and she made no move to get up. Looking worried, Hercules kneeled at her side. 'What is the matter? Did you not hear what I said?'

'I think my legs are broken,' she panted. 'They hurt— Ow! Don't touch them.'

Tim tried not to look at her legs, which lay at a funny angle. 'Can you carry her?' he asked Hercules. 'We have to get her to hospital. Err ... are there any hospitals in Ancient Greece?' Tim wasn't sure.

'The healing shrine at Epidaurus!' Hercules said, gently stroking his daughter's forehead. 'It is far, but I shall carry her. Day and night if necessary.'

'It may be necessary, but it will not be possible,' a smooth voice behind them said.

Tim spun around. Hera stood at the cave's entrance with a look of satisfaction on her face.

'YOU EVIL HAG!'

Hercules shouted, getting to his feet. 'You shall pay for hurting my daughter.'

'I didn't hurt her. You did! You made the boulder fall by breaking the column, you oaf,' Hera said, her lip curling. 'Anyway, it makes no difference. Your child has served her purpose.'

Hera turned her cold gaze onto Tim. He felt chilled by the icy hatred. 'As I hoped, she has brought Tim Baker to this cave. Now he shall stay here forever.'

The goddess looked back at Hercules. 'I warned you, did I not? Hand over the boy from the future or suffer the consequences. It seems you prefer to suffer. Then so be it – you shall all be trapped together!'

'Tim,' Zoe panted, pain etched on her face. 'Get out of here! Run!'

'Not without you.' Tim was adamant. He turned to Hera. 'Why are you so scared of the being forgotten?' he asked, remembering what the wise Athena had said to him about the queen goddess.

'Don't be ridiculous,' Hera sneered. 'I am not frightened of anything or anyone!' But the tense set of her jaw suggested otherwise.

Ever since Larry had played a trick on Hera with a mobile phone, she had directed her fear and anger at Tim. It seemed she wanted to rule forever, but what did that have to do with Tim?

'How does trapping me change anything?' Tim wanted to know.

'There is nothing to discuss.'

In one fluid, snake-like motion, Hera stepped outside. She clicked her fingers. The sound of boulders tumbling to the ground drowned out her laughter.

7

The interior of the cave was plunged
into darkness, with only a few beams
of light struggling through the gaps
between the rocks. The falling boulders
had sealed the entrance, cutting off their
escape. Zoe whimpered in pain and fear.
Hercules let out another giant bellow. The
sound echoed through the cave, making
the stalactites tremble. More dirt poured
down onto them.

'I think we need to be quiet,' Tim said, fighting to stay calm. 'We don't want the whole thing to collapse.'

Hercules seemed to see the sense in this, because he immediately fell silent. For a while all Tim could hear was the hero's ragged breathing and Zoe's soft sobbing.

'Is there another way out?' she asked shakily. 'These caves are full of tunnels. Maybe there's another exit.'

Although it was too dark to see properly, Tim knew that Zoe was in a bad way. It seemed to be taking all her energy just for her to speak. They had to get her out, and soon.

'I could try down that passage,' Tim said, staring into the darkness. He didn't fancy the idea of roaming around on his own, but what choice did they have? It would help if he had a torch ...

'No,' Hercules said firmly. 'The tunnels in these caves are like a labyrinth. It would not help Zoe if you became lost, Tim Baker. There must be another way for us to get out.'

'Such as?' Tim couldn't think of any.

'I will move those rocks with my bare hands. Stay with my daughter while I pluck those boulders out of our path.' Hercules sounded so sure of himself, Tim thought hopefully. There was still the problem of getting Zoe to a hospital – but one thing at a time.

Hercules shuffled to the entrance, cursing softly as he bumped his head on the low cave roof. With a lot of huffing and grunting, he started to push the boulders away. It took a long time, but finally he was able to clear an opening. 'That was not easy, my friend,' Hercules panted. 'Those rocks were wedged in tight.'

Tim looked at the cleared space. It wasn't very big. He could manage to squeeze through, but Hercules with Zoe in his arms? Not a chance.

'You must go and get help. I will continue to move the rocks while you are gone.'

Tim took one glance at Zoe's pale face and agreed. It would be quicker that way.

'Fetch the doctor Hippocrates. The last I heard, he was having an island holiday,' Hercules said. 'First you must go to Jason. Tell him to take you on his boat and to bring you and the doctor straight back. No joy riding. Go now.'

Tim paused only long enough to remove his jacket, fold it up, and place it under Zoe's head. She smiled weakly at him and closed her eyes. 'I'll be as quick as I can,' he promised.

Tim ran as fast as his legs could carry him. Luckily the wharf wasn't too far away. But what if Jason had grown tired of waiting? What if he'd left already? How on earth could Tim get to an island without a boat? He couldn't swim that far!

Don't worry about it unless you have to, Tim told himself. Just ... run.

And so he ran, all the way to the wharf. Tim nearly burst into tears of relief when he saw Jason climbing into the *Argonut*. It seemed that Tim was just in time - Jason was untying the ropes and preparing to sail.

'No! Wait!' Tim called, out of breath. 'I'm here!'

'You're lucky,' Jason said, putting down the coiled rope. 'Would you believe that no one else wanted to come for a spin? And on such as nice day as this!' He shook his head in disbelief. 'I'm glad you're so keen, though,' he said, looking at Tim's heaving chest.

'Yeah. Uh.' Tim couldn't say much more as he clambered unsteadily onto the boat, taking Jason's outstretched hand.

'So where to? Whaddya say to Mykonos? The party island!' Jason looked keenly out to sea. 'There's a great tailwind and I've got a few bros out there who'd love to see my new ride.'

Tim shook his head vigorously and tried to catch his breath. 'Hip– Hip–'

'Hooray! Yeah, I'm excited too. Let's go.'

'Hip-Hippocrates,' Tim managed to gasp. 'Must ... get the doctor.'

'Hippocrates?' Jason's eyebrows shot to the top of his forehead. 'I don't think he's into boats. All he cares about is sick people. Boring! He wouldn't know his jib from his boom. Crazy, right?'

'My friend's hurt,' Tim panted. 'She needs the doctor. Please.'

'I s'ppose,' Jason said, shrugging good-naturedly. 'I guess a ride is a ride, am I right? Hold on tight, little bro and off we go!'

Tim stared at the sparkling blue
water as the boat sliced through the
waves. The fresh, salty tang of the air
helped him catch his breath and made
his whole body tingle. Before long
he felt ready for action. If he wasn't
so worried about Zoe, he would have
really enjoyed the trip. They were
making good progress, but Tim wished
they could go even faster.

'Are we nearly there yet?' he asked Jason.

'Almost,' Jason replied.

He glanced sideways at Tim. 'You keep asking me. I get ya. You like going fast, huh? Me too.'

'Can't you do anything to get us there sooner?' Tim asked, looking at the sail. It was already billowing robustly, but surely there must be a way to speed things up. If only the Ancient Greeks had invented motor boats.

'Well I can, actually,' Jason said, puffing out his chest. 'You know Aeolus?'

Tim had to admit that he didn't.

'He's the Keeper of the Winds, man, where've ya been? If Aeolus is in a bad mood, he can blow up a hurricane and sink a ship. Sometimes he gets the sulk and there's no breeze at all. Then you have no choice but to whip out the oars and row. I reckon he's feeling all right today, though.'

Tim thought about it. 'So can we ask him to send more wind?'

Jason looked smug. 'Don't need to, do I? Hand me that bag.' He pointed to a leather pouch that was tucked safely near Tim's vase. 'Careful! Don't open it!'

'How come?' Tim edged carefully towards the pouch, trying to match his steps with the lift and swell of the boat. Although the bag looked full to bursting, it was as light as a balloon. 'What's inside?' he asked, handing it over.

'Wind, of course! What else would it be?' Jason rolled his eyes as he gripped the bag firmly. 'All the winds – every direction, every strength. We gotta be really careful, though, that we don't let the wrong ones out. If we do, they could blow us way off course. Who knows where we'd end up?'

Tim eyed the bag nervously. With Zoe in pain, they couldn't afford any mistakes. 'Maybe we should leave it then,' he said.

'Nah, don't worry. I know what I'm doing! A touch of a gentle West wind, that's what we need. Something to give us a bit more *oomph*.' Very delicately, Jason untied the string that held the bag closed. He peered into the narrow opening. 'That's the one,' he said as he squeezed the lip.

A great rushing sound came out of the bag and Jason pinched it shut again. He deftly tied the string back on. 'Woo hoo! Let it rip!' he cried, turning his face into the wind.

There was a sudden surge in speed, making Tim topple over backwards. He steadied himself with difficulty, then his jaw dropped open. Two big blue horses had materialised in front of the boat – on top of the sea! Their hooves kicked up giant sprays of foam. 'What are they?' he shouted over the sounds of the thundering water.

'Wind spirits,' Jason said, a grin plastered across his face. 'Aren't they beauties? They'll get us there in no time. Sit back and relax, little bro. We're in for some ride.'

Jason was right. Not long afterwards, the glistening sands of a mountainous island came into sight. They pulled the boat ashore and tied it up. Tim and Jason

searched for Hippocrates and found him sunning himself on the beach. The old man was lying on the sand, a piece of parchment covering his face. Gentle snoring issued from under the paper, fluttering its edges up and down.

'Are you sure that's him?' Tim asked, plucking at Jason's chiton.

'Course I am,' Jason said. 'Hey, Hippocrates. Wake up. Got a patient for you.'

The snoring stopped. 'Do you have an appointment?' the doctor asked without moving.

'Oh man, this is an emergency. Sailed here on my new ride, the *Argonut*,' Jason said importantly. 'You should have seen her cut through the waves! Sheer perfection.'

'An emergency? Why didn't you say so?' Hippocrates pulled himself to his feet with a soft moan. The old man was dressed in a crisp white chiton. He brushed sand out of his curly white beard and ran a hand over his balding head. His eyes sparkled with intelligence and his expression was kind. He squinted at Tim. 'Hmm, you don't look at all well. Very pale.' He placed a firm

hand on Tim's forehead. 'No fever. What appears to be the trouble?'

'It's not–' Tim tried to pull away.

'Don't worry, I won't hurt you,' the doctor said, tilting Tim's head back. He took a smooth piece of wood and placed it on Tim's tongue. 'Say aah.' He peered down Tim's throat.

'Aah ... no!' Tim wriggled out of the doctor's clasp. 'It's not me, it's my friend. Her legs were crushed by a big rock. She's in pain and looking really sick.'

'Oh dear, that does sound serious. Hmm, I'd better come right away. Does she have private health cover? Or is she on the Classical Health Service?'

'What? No. I don't know!'

'Never mind, we can sort out the
details later on. Now, where's my bag?'
Hippocrates hunted around until he found
a soft leather pouch lying half buried in
the sand. He picked it up and squared
his shoulders 'No time to waste, crush
fractures can be very serious. Take me to
your friend.'

Tim and Jason dashed back to the
boat and the old man hobbled after them
as fast as he could. He needed a bit of
help with boarding and Tim had to fight
not to show his impatience.

Soon they were
all in place, with
the doctor's
medical bag

stowed where it could not accidentally blow away. With a grin of pure delight, Jason set sail again.

There was no need for the bag of wind this time – a strong breeze was whipping the sail and the boat was moving rapidly through the water. Pleased that they'd get back to Zoe quickly, Tim gripped the side and watched the white clouds scudding across the sky. Suddenly, he grimaced and clapped a hand to his jaw. The cold sea air had made the pain in his tooth flare up again, and this time it was worse than ever.

'What's the problem?' Hippocrates asked, his piercing blue eyes focused on Tim.

'N-nothing.' Tim dropped his hand and flashed a weak smile. 'I'm f-fine.'

'Toothache?' the doctor asked shrewdly. 'I can relieve your pain.'

'You're not going to pull it out!' Tim yelped. 'Not without modern equipment!' He wished now that he'd seen a dentist after all.

'No, no,' Hippocrates soothed. 'Nothing of the sort. First do no harm!' He closed his eyes and considered. 'I can make you a poultice. Let me see, a simple pain-relieving antiseptic paste should suffice ... some ground cloves ... a bit of garlic ... yes. Get my bag.'

That didn't sound too bad. Tim fished around in the boat, his face screwed up from the pain. 'Got it.'

'Excellent. Now untie it, and we'll see what we've got.'

As soon as Tim tugged off the string, he knew something was wrong. He was expecting the comforting smell of medicinal herbs. Instead, it looked and sounded as if a volcano had erupted between his hands.

It felt as if the world were ending. Water
sprayed from all directions and the boat
was flung about violently. Tim clung on
as the wind howled and gibbered past his
ears. Squinting through the stinging sea
spray, he saw something that made his
jaw drop open. The big blue horses that
had sped them to the island had returned.
Once again, they were pulling the boat.
This time, however, they'd been joined by

other spirit horses. Even larger than the first ones, they were pulling the boat in all different directions. The wind spirits no longer galloped serenely through the water. They stampeded furiously, teeth bared, eyes flashing, manes whipping.

Tim's stomach dropped as he realised what had happened. He had opened the wrong bag! When he'd reached for Hippocrates' medicine bag, Tim had accidentally picked up the wind bag of Aeolus! All of the winds had been let loose at once, not just the gentle west wind. The wind spirits were bumping into each other, tussling and fighting for supremacy – and the *Argonut* was at the centre of the battle. The boat's sail couldn't take the rough whipping and was quickly reduced to streaming, loose shreds that flapped about violently.

'Keep low!' Jason shouted over the roaring winds. 'Hold tight!'

'What are we going to do?' Tim squealed.

'There's nothing we can do! We'll have to ride it out. Lucky, isn't it?'

Tim wasn't feeling particularly lucky at the moment. 'What is?' he asked.

'The fact that *I* built this boat.' Jason jerked a thumb at his chest. 'If it was anyone else, she'd be driftwood by now. And we'd have joined the sea nymphs.'

The boat did a gut-wrenching rise and fall but held together. Tim gulped. He supposed that they were fortunate. In a way.

'This clean sea air is most beneficial for the health.' Hippocrates spoke for the first time since the calamity occurred. The old man was sitting upright, looking unperturbed. Tim had expected a telling off for being careless, but instead the doctor's eyes glowed with enthusiasm. 'I advise you to open the lungs and take deep breaths. Like so.' He spread his arms out wide.

Tim opened his mouth to reply, but immediately wished he hadn't. The boat wrenched sharply starboard, almost capsizing. A wash of sea water flooded into his mouth. 'Pah!' he spat, feeling the bile rise in his throat.

'Saline rinses are good for toothache,' the doctor said, nodding encouragingly.

'Duck!' Jason shouted, as the ship's boom swung around, nearly hitting Tim in the back of the head.

Tim threw himself to the bottom of the boat, where the tossing and jolting felt less severe. There was also less to see. He decided to stay there.

■　■　■

Tim didn't know how long he'd lain motionless, eyes closed, trying to blot out the bucking and the swaying. But eventually the sea started to calm and the waves began to lap more gently at the boat. He pulled himself up gingerly and looked around. The horse-shaped wind spirits had gone. All that was left was

a gentle, natural breeze. The *Argonut*'s
shredded sail fluttered limply.

'Welcome back, little bro.' Jason
grinned at him. 'That was some ride, huh?'

'W-where are we?'

Jason shrugged. 'Who knows? We were
blown off course.'

Tim shaded his eyes with his hand and
looked out to sea. Not too far away was
a small, ragged island. Its shoreline was
cluttered by a jumble of sharp-looking rocks.

'Do you know that place?' he asked, pointing.

'Hard to say,' Jason replied. 'Many of these islands look alike, especially from this distance. I might be able to tell when we get closer. But cheer up! We can't be too far off course. As least we can still see land. If we were out in open ocean, that'd be different.'

Tim scanned the island's coast anxiously. There didn't seem to be anywhere safe to dock. 'Are we going to get off?'

'No point. I'll just get my bearings and then we'll sail home. This has been such a great day!' Jason shook his head in amazement. 'Can't wait to tell my bros about it. Man, they are gonna be mad that they missed out!'

Tim might have been more inclined to agree if it wasn't for the thought of Zoe waiting for him, pale and in pain. Now, because of his silly mistake, she was going to have to wait much longer. He bowed his head. If they got through this, he vowed he would never, ever, be so careless again!

'Hey.' Jason's startled voice cut through Tim's gloomy thoughts. 'Why've we stopped moving?'

It was true. Tim realised that the boat was no longer drifting towards the rocky island. It had even stopped bobbing up and down. Instead, it sat utterly still. How could that happen? The boat felt like it was on solid land, yet they were in the middle of the sea.

'Could it be caught on seaweed?' Hippocrates asked, tapping his fingertips together.

'Not this far out, no,' Jason said. 'It feels like something's holding – argh!'

Tim's shout joined Jason's as the boat suddenly jerked up into the air. The surface of the sea fell away as they went higher and higher. Shocked, Tim scuttled to the side of the boat and looked down. His jaw dropped open, and he had to blink several times to make sure he wasn't hallucinating.

A giant hand was holding the boat aloft, gripping it tightly in its palm.

The hand that gripped the boat was brownish yellow and it gleamed metallically in the sunlight. Tim had no idea what was happening. 'What is it?' he asked, his eyes fixed on the shiny fingers, which creaked as their grip tightened. The word 'robot' flashed through Tim's brain, but he quickly dismissed the idea. The Ancient Greeks didn't have robots ... did they?

'Oh man, not again,' Jason said, peering anxiously over the side of the boat. 'That thing had better not scratch my hull.'

'You've seen it before?' Tim asked, edging away from the gigantic thumb that had curled around the boat's edge.

'Not this one,' Jason answered. 'But I've seen another, yeah. They're all the same. Big ugly brutes that care nothing about fine workmanship.'

'Will it hurt us?' Tim wanted to know.

'Not if I've got a say in it!' Jason strode over to the thumb, grabbed it with both hands and pulled. 'Come on, help me loosen its grip. Doc, you go for that finger over there.'

Tim scuttled over to help Jason. The metal thumb was cold and wet and Tim's hands kept sliding off. He wiped them on his jeans to dry them.

'Dig in under the thumbnail,' Jason advised. 'We've gotta get it off us before—'

'Before what?' Tim asked, grappling with the monstrous thumbnail. It was sharp and jagged and he had to be careful not to cut his hands on it.

'Before that,' Jason answered, pointing at the sea.

As he spoke, a great splash came from the water below. Tim watched in disbelief as the top of a massive metal head appeared through the waves. Up popped a pair of eyebrows over hollow-looking eyes, then a narrow nose, thin mouth and square chin. Within seconds the head was followed by a gleaming neck, and shoulders broad enough to dock a ship on. Whatever it was kept rising until it was standing in water up to its waist.

'What on earth is that?' Tim yelped. If it was a robot, it was bigger than any that existed in the modern day.

'A giant bronze man, of course,' Jason said, staring at Tim as if he were dim. 'What does it look like? They are such a pain. One tried to smash my boat up when I was sailing to Crete.'

'H-how?' Tim tried to keep the tremor out of his voice. 'By picking you up and' – he gulped as he looked at the long drop below – 'throwing you back down again?'

'Nothing so gentle! No, it kept hurling rocks at us. Stupid brute. Don't they know how hard it is to get a glossy finish?' Jason glared at the bronze man. 'Oi. Put us down!'

'Who are you that dares to approach my island?' The bronze man's voice was shallow and tinny, and oddly mechanical.

As it spoke, it exposed a mouth full of pointed metal teeth.

'They call me Jason. And if you've scratched my boat, dude, I'm going straight to my lawyers. It's brand new; get what I'm saying? I hope you've got insurance!'

'Jason.' The bronze man's face drew closer, until its sharp-edged teeth were just a few metres away. 'Not Jason of Jason and the Argonauts?'

Tim found it impossible to read the expression on the blank metallic face. Was it angry? Surprised? Wary? There were no muscles that could frown or smile or sneer, just a jumble of interconnected panels. It was like trying to read the feelings of a car or a computer. Even the bronze man's voice was flat and emotionless.

'The same,' Jason said, looking pleased. 'You've heard of me, huh?'

'You killed my brother.' The heavy eyelids creaked as they clanked shut and opened again. 'His name was Talos.'

'Oh him! Well, he shouldn't have chucked rocks at my ride, should he?' Jason shrugged. 'Anyway, it wasn't me that got him. It was my girl, Medea.'

'You shouldn't have approached my brother's island. He was its guardian, charged to defend it to the death. Just as I, Brountzos, am the guardian of this one.' The giant head swivelled to look at the small island.

'That piddly little thing?' Jason glanced at the rocky shore with contempt. 'It's hardly worth the effort. Tell you what – put us down and we'll go away. If my ride's not damaged, we'll say no more about it.'

'You forget. I am duty bound to avenge the death of my brother.'

'Oh yeah? Well then I have to avenge the damage to my first ride, the *Argo*.'

Jason and Brountzos locked gazes and gritted their teeth. They seemed to be engaged in a battle of wills, leaving Tim totally bewildered.

'What are they talking about?' he asked Hippocrates, who had moved beside him.

'You don't know the story?' The doctor raised an eyebrow. 'After they retrieved the Golden Fleece, Jason and the Argonauts sailed past the island of Crete. The bronze man Talos emerged from the sea and tried to stop the *Argo* from landing. Jason's ex-wife Medea was on the ship with him. She was a brilliant woman, who worked out how to destroy the monster.'

Jason broke eye contact with Brountzos long enough to flash them a smile. 'Yeah, my ex knew nothing about boats, but she worked out how to beat that guy.'

'What did she do?' Apart from waiting for it to rust, Tim thought the metal man looked impossible to defeat.

'Bronze men have only one vein that runs through their entire body,' Hippocrates said, with the air of a professor talking to a student. 'This vein is bound shut by a nail. If one can find this nail and remove it, the bronze man will bleed to death. A very inefficient system, is it not? No clotting mechanism at all.' The doctor shook his head disapprovingly.

'Yeah, Bronzey,' Jason snapped. 'So watch it!'

'Brountzos.' The bronze man corrected him. Did Tim detect a note of irritation in the monster's voice? 'You do not frighten me, tiny human. My brother's nail was plain for all to see: an unfortunate oversight. However, mine is so well hidden that I shall offer you a challenge. If you can find my nail, I will let you go.'

'And if we c-can't?' Tim asked.

The reply was abrupt. 'If you can't, I will eat you.'

11

Tim shook himself and tried to
concentrate. It wasn't easy when
something was threatening to turn you
into lunch. 'Wh-where was Talos' nail?' he
asked Hippocrates.

The doctor frowned. 'By his ankle, I
believe.'

Tim looked at the sea. He couldn't see
the bottom. 'How are we supposed to get
down there? It's too deep.'

'We can trick him into taking us with him onto dry land,' Jason said under his breath. 'As long as he sets us down gently ...'

But the doctor was shaking his head. 'You forget. That's where *Talos'* nail was. This one claims that his is in a different location. One that is harder to find.'

The three fell silent as they scrutinised Brountzos carefully. There was no sign of a nail, a screw, or any sort of plug. All Tim could see was smooth metal interlocking panels.

'What are bronze men, exactly?' he asked. 'Are they alive or are they machines?'

'Bronze men were created by Hephaistos, the blacksmith god,' Hippocrates answered, not taking his eyes away. 'As to whether they are alive ...' He shrugged. 'It depends on your definition of life. Does it have emotions? Does it feel pain? I cannot say.'

Tim hesitated. 'But if we pull the nail out it'll die, right?'

'Oh yes,' the doctor said. 'If one drains out its metallic life blood, it will die.'

Tim went silent.

'We have no choice, little bro,' Jason said through gritted teeth. 'It's us or him. Keep looking for that nail.'

But it was already too late. 'I am growing tired of this, you are too slow!' Brountzos said, baring his fang-like teeth and moving the boat steadily towards his expressionless face.

Heart pounding, Tim stared into the gaping mouth and froze. Suddenly, he saw it! One of the bronze man's teeth looked different to the rest. Rather than being sharply pointed at the tip, it was cylindrical, like a tin can. It had to be the nail. All Tim needed to do was climb out of the boat, walk along the bronze man's arm, put his arms around the nail and tug ...

But to kill it? Could he bring himself to do it? Tim knew it was a monster, but it kind of looked human. It was upset about its brother. 'Would you take out the nail?' he asked Hippocrates worriedly. 'If you saw it?'

'First do no harm,' the doctor answered, pressing his lips together. 'Killing is against my vow as a man of medicine.'

'Listen, bro, if you see the nail, then do it. Don't mess about.' Jason's voice was firm. 'I don't care if it's alive or not – I care if *we're* alive or not! And my boat, of course.' He patted the wood. 'She's suffered enough.'

It wasn't just his life on the line, it was Jason's and Hippocrates' … and Zoe's.

Tim made up his mind. Without a word he clambered out of the boat and onto the bronze man's hand. The wet metal was slippery and he nearly slid off into the ocean below. Wobbling, Tim flung out his arms to regain his balance. Trying not to think too much about what he was doing, he squatted low then pushed himself off the bronze hand as hard as he could. For

one terrifying moment he was leaping
through the air, then he managed to hook
himself onto the metal man's lip.
He pulled himself gingerly to his feet
and stood on Brountzos' glistening
tongue. Tim reached out and touched the
cylindrical tooth.

'It's here,' Tim said, his voice echoing in the metal chamber. 'Let us go or I will pull it out!'

'Urgh.' Brountzos' groan was deafeningly loud. Tim clapped his hands over his ears. Suddenly he was falling, plummeting faster and faster. He gasped as his back slammed into the boat and he skidded across the deck. He'd been spat out!

'You win,' the bronze man said, its voice flat. 'I honour my promises. Go now and do not return. If I ever see you again, I will eat you without hesitation.'

With that, Brountzos hurled the boat away from his island as hard as he could. Tim and his friends sailed so far through the air it felt like they were flying.

The boat smashed into the water hard, throwing up enormous sprays of foam that drenched them head to foot. Tim was sure that the boat would capsize, but after a few heart-stopping moments it stabilised itself.

'Man, what a ride,' Jason breathed, pulling himself to his feet and caressing the boat lovingly. 'Isn't she great?'

■ ■ ■

Tim was relieved that the trip back to the wharf was brief. In his fury, Brountzos had hurled them almost all the way back home. Sure, they had to row like crazy to make up for the shredded sail, but at least they were no longer lost. 'Thank the gods,' he found himself murmuring, even though he wasn't sure which ones he meant.

'Take your stuff with you,' Jason said when they docked. He pointed to Tim's vase and the model boat. 'I'm gonna fix the sail, then I'm off again. There's still time to set off for Mykonos before it gets dark. It's been good sailing with ya, little bro. Join me any time!'

Tim grappled with the seawater-spattered vase and raft as he disembarked. Hippocrates picked up his medical bag and followed. Now that they were finally close to helping Zoe, Tim was growing more impatient. He broke into an awkward run, the vase bumping against his chest as he jogged along.

'Zoe! Hercules!' Tim called as he approached the cave. He hoped that Hercules had been able to clear more boulders from the entrance. There was no way the ageing doctor would be able to squeeze his way through the small hole.

'Tim Baker, you are here at last!' The relief in the hero's voice was plain. Hercules appeared at the cave entrance, which fortunately was now completely clear. A pile of discarded boulders lay near the flower beds.

'I'm sorry we took so long,' Tim spluttered, trying to catch his breath. 'How is she?' He plonked the vase and the model boat onto the ground. Relieved of his burden, he ran the rest of the way to the cave, ignoring the stitch in his side.

'She is in pain,' Hercules said, his face grim. 'My child is very brave.'

'Lead me to her,' Hippocrates said.

Hercules took the old man by the arm and led him through the cave to where Zoe lay, her eyes shut and her face pale.

'Oh dearie me,' the doctor murmured. He knelt next to the girl and gently touched her legs. 'Hmm.'

'Ow!' Zoe whimpered, opening her eyes at the touch. Her entire body trembled.

'Stay still, my child. I will not hurt you.' Hippocrates reassured Zoe before continuing his task. 'Oh dear me. Tch.'

Hercules shuffled from foot to foot while his daughter was examined. Tim knew it was taking all of the hero's self-control to not explode with impatience. 'What?' Hercules asked, when the doctor finally stopped tutting and tongue clicking and pushed himself back to his feet.

Hippocrates shook his head and frowned. 'I'm afraid it's bad news.'

Tim looked at Zoe. What was
Hippocrates talking about? He knew
Zoe's legs were injured, but the doctor
made the problem sound far worse than
it looked. Her legs didn't seem *that* bad.
There was no blood, no obviously broken
bones. She was very pale, however, and
sweating heavily. Hercules stood beside
Tim and gripped his shoulder. Tim
winced but said nothing.

'Her legs were crushed by the boulder,' the doctor said. 'There is considerable bleeding beneath the skin. Worse than that, she might have irreversible damage to the underlying nerves and muscles.' Hippocrates paused when he saw Hercules' blank expression. 'I'm trying to say it might be permanent. My fear is that she may not walk again.'

The hero's jaw dropped. Tim had never before seen him at a loss for words.

'It's not definite, mind you,' Hippocrates hastened to add. 'She may still recover. The fact that you lifted the boulder off her so quickly gives her the best chance. And the fact that she feels pain shows she hasn't lost sensation in her legs. But, as I said, her condition is serious.'

Tim wished he could scoop Zoe up in his arms and take her to the best hospital in London. 'Isn't there anything you can do?' he asked, hands clenching. He was starting to realise how hard it was to live in Ancient Greece.

'She needs to go to a temple of the healer-god Asclepius, where she will be given the care she needs,' the doctor said. 'There is nothing I can do for her here, apart from apply a few poultices to ease her discomfort.'

'Are there any of these temples nearby?' Tim asked. 'We can carry her there!'

The doctor shook his head. 'The nearest is several days' walk over rough terrain.

Even if you had a chariot, the jolting might do more harm than good.'

'My vase!' Tim said. 'I can use it to fly her there.' It would be difficult, but he'd manage it somehow.

'Flying would be the worst thing for her,' Hippocrates said firmly. 'The change in air pressure, the constant buffeting. No. You will have to treat her in her own home.'

'Tell me what to do,' Hercules said, his voice hoarse with emotion. 'I shall give her the finest care a father can provide.'

Tim bowed his head. It hurt him to see his friends in pain. The thought of Zoe never walking again made his head spin. It didn't seem real! She was always so lively, so animated. If only there was something he could do. He wondered what the treatment was like in his day. Then he brightened. Maybe he could go home and ask a modern doctor! There must be something ... some equipment ... some medicine he could bring back ...

'Argh!' Tim suddenly shouted, face-palming himself.

'Do not despair, my friend,' Hercules said, glancing at Tim. 'I am touched that you feel so upset, but we must stay positive and

hope for the best. Beating yourself up will not help.'

'I'm not. I've had an idea. Oh wow, I am so stupid!'

'Your idea is that you are stupid?' Hercules clicked his tongue. 'Tim Baker, I do not think that your idea will help Zoe very much.'

Tim didn't bother to explain. Instead he turned to the doctor. The sense of urgency was making him tremble. Why hadn't he thought of this before? 'Would the Golden Fleece cure her?' he asked. He crossed his fingers that it wasn't too late.

Hippocrates stroked his beard thoughtfully. 'Of course. The fleece will cure anything. But how do you propose to obtain it, young man? We could have asked Jason what he did with it, I suppose, but he will be long gone by now.'

'Arachne's gloves.' Zoe tried to pull herself upright, her face twisted with pain. She was referring to the gloves that Arachne had made out of the Golden Fleece. 'But she only made one pair. We can't get another.'

'I've still got them, remember? At home!'

A weak smile flitted across Zoe's face as she sank back down. 'Of course. I should have remembered.'

'You and me both.' Tim grinned. 'I'm so sorry! I'll go right now and get them.'

'You have the vase?' Zoe asked.

'It's outside! Hold on, I'll be back in a sec.' Without bothering to explain to the astonished-looking Hippocrates, Tim raced outside. He dashed to his vase and picked it up. 'Oh vase, take me home. And hurry!'

The trip home took the same time it always did, but to Tim it felt incredibly slow. Finally, the vase landed in his bedroom. Hitting the ground running, Tim darted to his chest of drawers and rifled around in his sock drawer. 'Gloves, gloves,' he muttered. 'Come on. Ah. Got you!'

Thrusting the Golden Fleece gloves into his pocket, Tim stepped back towards the vase. He was just about to grab it when he remembered something. The gift for the Grey Women! If he didn't take them a gift by sunset, they'd release a plague! Grateful that he'd remembered in time, Tim dashed into the bathroom to fetch a tube of toothpaste and a toothbrush.

'Oi, Cinderella! Watcha doing?'

Tim had forgotten that Leo was still at his house, where they were meant to be making the raft together. Tim spluttered with impatience. He didn't want to deal with this now! All he wanted was to get back to Zoe and make her better.

'Brushing my teeth. What does it look like I'm doing?' Tim waved the toothbrush in the air.

'What have ya done with the raft?' Leo asked, narrowing his eyes suspiciously.

'You'll see. I won't be long.'

Tim ran to his bedroom. He slammed the door shut and wedged a chair under the knob.

That should stop Leo following him. Heart thumping, Tim grasped the vase's handles. 'Oh vase,' he said, 'take me to Perseus' cave.'

In the split
second before the golden
mist fell, Tim saw the door
get wrenched open. He groaned. He'd
forgotten that it opened outwards! Leo's
freckled face poked through the doorway
and twisted in his direction. His eyes
bulged and his mouth formed a comical
'O' shape.

Oh well. There was no time to worry
about that now.

Tim urged the soaring vase to
go faster. It made no difference, but
nagging made him feel better. The
vase dropped him just outside the cave.
Dumping it on the ground, Tim dashed
inside. 'Got them!'

'Excellent.' Hippocrates took the gloves from Tim and pulled them on. The doctor kneeled next to Zoe. 'Relax, child. This won't hurt at all,' he said, and gently touched her crushed legs.

Tim watched in awe as the colour returned to Zoe's face. One moment she was lying there, pale and in pain. The next moment she was sitting up, rosy cheeked and smiling. It was incredible.

'The Golden Fleece will cure your toothache, too,' Hippocrates said, pulling off the gloves and handing them back to Tim. 'Remember that the next time you have a flare up.'

Tim grinned. He would certainly remember! It was better than the dentist. And he'd make sure to take the gloves with him everywhere he went ... just in case.

'I must be going now.' The doctor got to his feet with difficulty and turned to Hercules. 'Anything else while I'm here? A quick check of your four humours? I suspect you have an excess of yellow bile, which leads to aggression. I may have some herbs ... No? In that case, there is the matter of my bill ...'

Leaving the doctor and the hero to sort out the details, Tim scurried over to Zoe. She was already back on her feet and bouncing around as if making up for lost time.

'Let's keep one each,' he said, handing Zoe one of the gloves. 'Then we've both got some fleece if we ever need it.'

'Thanks,' Zoe said gratefully. 'And thanks for helping me.' She gave Tim a hug. She didn't let go until he pulled away, embarrassed.

'I'd better go now,' Tim said awkwardly. 'I wish I could stay longer, but there's something I need to do.'

Tim promised to tell his friend all about the adventures he'd had later. Then he left, checking he still had the Grey Women's gift in his pocket as he did so. He stepped out of the cave and tucked the model boat under his arm. He only hoped he wasn't too late. Grabbing the vase, Tim said, 'Oh vase, take me to the hut of the three Grey Women.'

■ ■ ■

The sun was low in the sky when he landed outside the hut. He peered at the red-streaked clouds anxiously. Hopefully the Grey Women had decided to wait until the sun had set fully before carrying out their threat to release the plague on Hercules' town. Although he and Zoe had the Golden Fleece gloves, he didn't know whether they could save a whole town. Tim had learned about the Great Plague of London at school, and he shivered.

A rasping cough made Tim jump. Had it started already? He pushed open the door to the hut. 'Don't do it! I'm here!' he gasped.

'Who are – oh yes,' the old woman with the eye said. 'You arrived just in time. We were about to release the plague, but decided to have a little snack first. Stupid grape pip got stuck in my throat.' She finished clearing her throat. 'That's what happens when someone else is hogging the tooth!' She glared at the other woman.

'Did he bring the gift?' the one with the tooth asked.

'Here it is,' Tim said. He held out the toothpaste and the brush. 'Give me the tooth and I'll show you what to do.'

'What has he brought?'

The single bloodshot eye swivelled around then focused on Tim's hand. 'It appears to be some kind of pungent unguent. And a device with which to apply it.'

The woman with the tooth broke out into a grin. 'Come here then, my boy, and brush my tooth! Save it from destruction.' She bared her single tooth at him.

Tim backed away. He could smell

her breath from where he was standing, and did not intend to get any closer. He waited until she agreed to hand it over then showed them how to brush the tooth.

'This is a whitening toothpaste,' he explained. 'Do this every morning and every night.' The eyeball rotated around and around, following his circular brush strokes. It was starting to make him feel queasy again. 'You're not going to release the plague, are you?' he asked worriedly.

'No, no, we are satisfied with this gift. Mmm, it smells so minty! Does it come in other flavours? How about goat's cheese?'

'Hey,' Tim said, remembering. 'Don't you always speak in rhymes? You did before. Now you're speaking normally.'

'Oh, we got bored of that.' She waved her hand dismissively. 'Tomorrow we might try talking in sentences that run backwards. Think you do what?'

Tim shrugged. He didn't want to get involved. As soon as he'd shown them how to rinse, he handed back the tooth and left. He could hear the women cackling happily as he picked up his vase and ordered it to take him home.

Pleasing the three Grey Women had been a cinch. Now for the hard part: Leo.

As Tim had expected, Leo was waiting for him when he reappeared in his room.

'Caught ya, Cinderella!' Leo hooted when the golden mist cleared. 'You'd better tell me what's going on, or I'll fix you up.' He raised his beefy fists threateningly.

Tim backed away from the bully. He was worn out after his adventure, and in no mood for a confrontation. 'Don't come near me. I'm warning you!'

'Yeah? What are you gonna do?' Leo sneered. 'Set your non-existent pet snake on me? Or maybe that spider?' He was referring to one of their previous encounters.

Tim wished he could send the giant spider Arachne to pay Leo a visit. That would shut him up.

'You told me that vase had a snake in it,' Leo said accusingly, pointing at it. 'But instead you used it to – what did you use it to do? I saw you pick it up and – and there was this mist – and you vanished – and then you came back again!'

Tim decided that attack was the best form of defence. 'Yeah, right,' he snorted. He put the vase down behind him, out of Leo's reach. 'I think someone's being watching too much TV. Mixing up real life with movies now, are we?'

'Don't give me that.' Leo stepped forward and grabbed a fistful of Tim's shirt. 'You tell me what's going on or you'll be sorry!' His eyes bulged as he spotted the model boat, which was still tucked under Tim's arm. 'Hey, how did you do that?' he spluttered, releasing Tim's shirt. 'You've only been gone a few minutes. Give it here!' Leo snatched the miniature *Argonut* and turned it over in his hands. 'Is this our raft?' he asked incredulously.

Tim cleared his throat. 'Yeah. Well. Sort of. It'll have to do.'

'It's so cool,' Leo breathed. 'But how? You couldn't even tie a few sticks together before. This looks like it came from the shops. Better, even.' His eyes narrowed dangerously, and he looked Tim up and down. He was probably taking in Tim's tousled hair and still-damp clothes – a contrast to his neat appearance before he'd left. 'Tell me what's going on, Cinderella. Or so help me, I'll …'

'You'll what?'

'I'll smash your stupid vase. Then you won't be able to do – whatever it is you do!' Leo made a sudden lunge towards the vase.

Tim nearly toppled over but managed to get to it first. 'If you touch it,' he

hissed, cradling the vase in his arms, 'I'll – I'll …'

'YOU'LL WHAT?'

Tim was trying to think of something smart to say when his mother walked in.

'How are you going with the raft, boys?' she asked, wiping her hands on her apron. 'Nearly done? Leo will have to head home soon, I'm afraid. I've got a friend coming over for dinner and I need to get ready.'

What she really meant, Tim realised, was that her boyfriend was coming over and she didn't want Leo to see him. Larry was a teacher at their school and their relationship was still a secret.

Mum glanced at Tim, who was clinging to the vase as if his life depended on it. 'What are you doing with that?' Her eyes widened. 'Hey, how did you fix all the cracks?' Mum ran her hands over the vase's smooth surface. 'It looks as good as it did before it broke. Better, even. So shiny. Hmm.'

Tim didn't like the sound of that hmm. His mother's eyes gleamed.

'Err ...' he said.

'You know, I think we could sell it after all,' she breathed. 'Think of the money this would bring. I could quit my second job straight way! How marvellous.'

Tim felt as if an electric shock had passed through his body. He couldn't bear

it if his vase were sold. How could he
give up his adventures in Ancient Greece?
What would Hercules and Zoe think if he
never turned up again? They'd worry that
something had happened to him.

'Um,' he said, not wanting to reveal
anything in front of Leo, 'I think we need

to talk about this later. When you're not busy.' He sent her a piercing gaze that said *please don't do anything yet – we can't possibly sell it.*

His mother didn't seem to get the message, however. 'Wonderful! I had a few people interested before I told them it was no longer for sale.' She rubbed her hands together. 'I might give them a call.'

'No wait—'

Mum turned to Leo. 'Is your grandmother coming to fetch you, or are you going home by yourself? I can give her a call her now and ask her to come, if you like.'

'No. I'll go. I'll take the raft with me.' Leo clumped down the stairs and looked back up at Tim on the landing. 'See ya at school. Then you can tell me all about the vase – that you used to have!' With a nasty chuckle, he let himself out, slamming the door behind him.

Tim's mother smiled. 'Right. Well, I'll make those calls first, then I'll set the table. Larry will be here in half an hour.'

'Mum!' Tim sounded more desperate than he intended.

'Yes, dear?'

'Can you please not call the buyers? Not right now. I – I need to talk to you first.'

'Well ... I suppose one more day won't make any difference,' she agreed. 'But really, Tim, this way I get to be at home

with you.' She stroked his cheek. 'Isn't
that worth more than some old pot?'

How could he say no? Tim stood rooted
to the spot, stricken.

'I'll go set up for dinner,' Mum said. 'I
made lasagne. Smells good, doesn't it?'

Tim nodded, his
glued-on smile
dripping off his

face as Mum went down the stairs. While he waited for Larry to arrive, Tim paced up and down in his bedroom. He decided to tell the teacher what Mum was planning and ask for his help. Tim wasn't sure how such a request would go down, though. Maybe Larry would even agree that it should go. What could he say to convince them?

His mind was in turmoil and his head swam. Maybe Mum would find a buyer right now, tonight. Maybe the vase would be gone before the end of the day! He might not even get a chance to say goodbye to his friends. They might think he'd forgotten them!

Tim couldn't bear it. He would never, ever, forget how special his trips to the past had been. When he was with Zoe, he was no longer an ordinary kid. Together they fought monsters and faced up to the gods. Together, they were something special.

No, he had to go back. Even if it was only to say goodbye.

Tim grabbed the vase's handles. 'Oh vase, take me to Zoe's house,' he said, for what he hoped wasn't the last time.

■ ■ ■

The sun had almost fully set when Tim found himself on Zoe's doorstep. The red clouds had turned purple. They hung low and heavy in the sky, like swollen bruises. Tim didn't think it was too late to visit. He knocked on the door.

Heavy footsteps sounded in the courtyard, then the door was flung open. Hercules stood before him, munching on a handful of small, dark yellow fruits. The hero's eyebrows drew together as he looked at Tim. 'What do you want?'

Tim was taken aback. He was used to a much friendlier welcome. 'I, err ...'

'Are you selling amphorae?' the hero glanced at Tim's vase. 'No thank you, we already have some.' He started to close the door.

'Wait!' Tim yelped. 'I've come to say hello! To you and to Zoe.'

A look of anger crossed the hero's face. 'How do you know my daughter? Who are you, who comes to people's houses at night-time, and in such strange clothing?

Are you a barbarian?'

'I – I ... it's me! Tim Baker!'

'A baker? We don't need any bread.'

Tim couldn't believe this was happening.
He heard scampering footsteps as Zoe ran
to the door. Tim looked at her, relieved.

'Zoe! Can you tell your Dad that I'm me?'

The girl looked at him uncertainly. 'Who are you? How do you know my name?' She glanced at Hercules. 'Who is he, Dad?'

Tim shuffled from foot to foot. Was this some kind of practical joke? He didn't think it was very funny. 'Come on, guys, let me in. I need to talk to you. It's important.'

Tim stepped forward, only to be barred by his friend's solid arm. Tim had never seen him look so angry. 'I am telling you nicely,' Hercules growled. 'Go now, whoever you are. And do not come back! If I ever see you around here again ...' He let the words hang menacingly in the air between them.

Tim stepped back in shock. The door slammed in his face. He stood for a minute, staring at it. He didn't understand what

was happening. Should he knock again?
Or would that just make Hercules even
angrier? His mind reeling, Tim needed to
think this through.

'Oh vase,' he said, his
voice dripping with
misery. 'Take
me home.'

Look out for Tim's next ADVENTURE!

~~HOPELESS HEROES~~

CIRCE'S BEASTLY FEAST

STELLA TARAKSON

Sweet Cherry

Tim Baker couldn't believe it. There must have been a mistake. How could his friends in Ancient Greece have forgotten him? After all they'd been through! It didn't make sense.

Except … maybe it did, Tim thought moodily, staring at his bedroom wall. Maybe Hercules had decided that he couldn't forgive Tim. Not after his daughter got hurt on their last adventure.

Hercules had forbidden him from visiting them once before. The hero had told Tim straight out that he didn't want Zoe to get involved in dangerous adventures. This time was different, though. Hercules didn't seem to know who Tim was. He didn't even recognise the vase, which had been his prison for thousands of years. How could that be? Even Zoe had said she didn't know Tim. And *she* wouldn't pretend. She never held back on her feelings. If she was upset with someone she would say so. Loudly and clearly.

What was going on?

Tim stared at the old Greek vase, at the picture of Hercules wrestling a

bull, at the ancient
writing that spoke of
the vase's mystery
and magic. A lump
formed in his throat.
Hercules had been
trapped in the vase by
the queen goddess Hera.
By accidentally breaking
it, Tim had set the hero free. That was
when it had all started – the friendships,
the adventures, the chance to do amazing
things. And maybe …

… maybe this was where it would all end.

During one of Tim's visits to the past, the messenger god Hermes had repaired the glued-together vase. He'd made it look as good as new, but now Mum wanted to sell it. Because the vase was so old, it was very valuable. Selling it would give her enough money to quit her second job. And then that would be that: no more adventures.

Tim had thought that Hercules and Zoe would worry about him if he never returned, so he'd decided to go back and tell them that the vase was being sold. Only to discover that they didn't know who he was!

Tim wished there was someone he could talk to about his problem. The only person who knew his secret was Mum's boyfriend, Larry. But he had already made it clear that he didn't think Tim should return to Ancient Greece. It was too dangerous. If Tim went to Larry for advice, the teacher would simply sit back, cross his long legs and confirm Tim's deepest fears. His Greek friends thought that he should stay away too. Perhaps this was their way of saying goodbye.

Still, Tim couldn't quite believe it. There *had* to be an explanation for their strange behaviour – but what?

Maybe he could ask the Pythia! Tim grinned as the thought occurred to him. The oracle should be able to help. After all, it was her job to answer people's questions. Tim remembered the time he'd gone to her for advice – that had turned out well in the end. Tim frowned. Last time the Pythia had insisted on a tribute. But what could he give her? Without Zoe's help, he had no idea what a suitable tribute might be. Besides, all the Pythia's

screeching and wailing had given him a headache. Maybe he should go straight to the source of her information – bypass the oracle and ask the god who spoke through her.

APOLLO.

He hadn't been too friendly last time, but that might have been because he'd been preparing for a gig. The god of prophecy was also the god of music – punk music, to be precise. The angry young god was anti-everything and way too interested in vomit. Still, Tim couldn't think of a better idea.

He gripped the magic vase's handles. 'Oh vase, take me to Apollo.'

Tim landed on the steps of a glistening black temple. Clutching the vase to his chest, he crept between the towering columns. Aggressive guitar-like music filled the air and Tim had to shout to be heard over it.

'APOLLO? MR APOLLO, SIR?'

The strumming stopped, and a crotchety voice called from the temple's dark interior. 'Who the Hades is that? Can't you see I'm busy?'

Squinting, Tim saw the slim god sitting cross-legged on the floor. He was holding a lyre.

'Can I talk to you for a minute?' Tim took a step closer.

'Are you deaf? I said I'm busy!' Apollo's mohawk bristled.

'I only—'

'I've written a new song, but I can't think of a rocking title! I'm sick to the Styx of trying! So get lost.'

Tim thought quickly. 'If I can come up with a title for you, will you help me?'

Apollo sniffed. 'Maybe. But it better be good! Here, listen.' The god burst out into a sudden, jerky tune with loud screeching lyrics that made no sense. Tim tried very hard not to clap his hands over his ears. When Apollo

finished, he glared at Tim expectantly. 'Well?'

'Awesome! It'll be a hit,' Tim chirped, hoping the god couldn't read minds. 'How about you call it, err …' He racked his brain for something sufficiently revolting. 'Erm … *Rolling in the Dung Heap?*

'That's a worse idea than *living* in a dung heap! Get out.'

'Okay, okay.' Tim raised his hands in defeat. 'How about *Blame It on the Bogie?* Or, um, *Let It Pee?*

'*Let It Pee.*' Apollo said the words slowly, trying them out. 'Yeah, sick!' Grinning, he scribbled the title on a scrap of parchment. 'Right, you've got ten seconds.'

The words tumbled over each
other as Tim hastened to explain his
problem.

Apollo curled his pierced lip.
'Sounds simple to me. I reckon you
went to the wrong time.'

'W-what do you mean?'

'I mean, phlegm-face, you might have gone back to *before* they'd met you.'

'Hey, yeah! Maybe.'

Tim brightened. It made sense! Normally the vase took him to a time that followed on naturally from the previous one. Maybe something had gone wrong. He had said "take me *back* to Zoe's house." Had it mistakenly taken him too far back? It was possible. Relief washed over him.

'Thanks! I'll try again.'

'Yeah.' Apollo went back to his lyre, muttering. '*Let It Pee* ...'

Tim had to make sure that the vase landed at the right time, and not just in the right place. 'Oh vase, take me to Zoe's house,' he said. 'Make sure it's right after her legs were cured by the Golden Fleece gloves.' He thought some more. 'Actually, make it the next morning, a bit after breakfast.' Tim didn't want to turn up too late at night. Besides, his friend needed to recover from her ordeal.

The vase seemed to understand what Tim was saying. It waited until he finished giving his instructions before it lifted him into the air.

Tim landed neatly on Zoe's doorstep. The sun was rising, and the air was cool and fresh. Tim felt hopeful. He put the vase down and knocked on the door. Hercules opened it. By the look of it, the hero was still eating his breakfast. He was chewing, and holding a handful of dark yellow fruits.

'YOU AGAIN!'

Hercules growled. 'Why have you returned? I told you last night – we do not want to buy your amphora.' He glanced scornfully at the vase at Tim's feet.

Tim's stomach lurched. How could this be happening? The vase hadn't taken him to the wrong time after all. 'Why don't you recognise me? We're friends. I know you, and Zoe, and your wife Agatha–'

Hercules' eyes bulged alarmingly. 'Who asked you to come here? What do you want? Are you a thief? A kidnapper?' He glared up and down the street. 'Where is your accomplice?'

'I don't have one!' Tim resisted the urge to clutch at Hercules' chiton. 'I'm not out to hurt you or your family … I'm Tim Baker. From the future. Remember? Hera trapped you in this vase and you were there for thousands of years. I broke it and set you free.'

'What nonsense is this?' Hercules scoffed. 'I have never been trapped in any type of ceramic pot or vessel.' He planted his beefy hands on his hips. 'And how could you say such awful things about

Hera? That wonderful woman is like a mother to me. If you were not a child, I would hurl you into the Underworld for spreading such vicious lies!'

Now Tim knew something was seriously wrong. Hera … wonderful? Like a mother? How could Hercules not remember all the times the wicked goddess had tried to capture them?

'Leave now and don't come back.' Hercules added, 'Next time, I will not be so merciful.' With that, he slammed the door in Tim's face.

Blinking rapidly, Tim picked up his vase and turned away. He had

no idea where to go. Somewhere quiet, where he could sit on his own and think. Why had his friends rejected him and sided with their enemy? It didn't make sense. A tear trickled down his cheek, but he felt too miserable to wipe it away.

Heads turned as Tim walked down the street. He felt out of place in his modern-day outfit of jeans and a T-shirt. Zoe's mother Agatha had made him his very own chiton, but Tim obviously couldn't go and ask for it now. For the first time, he felt as if he didn't belong in Ancient Greece.

'Hello there, little buddy.'
Tim swivelled around at the sound
of the familiar
voice. It was
Hermes, the
messenger god.
The wings on
his cap and
sandals flapped
in greeting.

'You know
who I am?' Tim
asked.

'Course I do!'
Hermes tipped
his head to the
side. 'Shouldn't I,

Tim Baker? Is this some sort of guessing game? Kids from the future have a weird idea of fun.'

'No, it's just …' Tim hesitated. He'd never been too sure about whether he could trust Hermes. There were times when the young god seemed to help Tim, but at other times it was harder to tell. In any case, there was no denying that Hermes was Hera's servant. He was also the god of thieves and liars, which Zoe was always quick to point out.

Zoe. Tim felt a pang of misery, and before he knew it, the words came gushing out. 'It's just that nobody else seems to know who I am.' He put the vase down with a sigh.

'That's odd.' Hermes frowned. He sat on a low wall and gestured for Tim to join him. 'Tell me everything.'

So Tim did. It took a while to get the whole story out, but by the end of it Hermes was nodding. 'Yes, yes, I think I see.'

'What?'

'They're upset that Zoe got injured,' Hermes said, his eyes wide and round. 'Can't blame them, really. Hercules is trying to protect his kid. I think all this forgetting business is just an act.'

This echoed Tim's first thoughts. There was something that still didn't make sense though. 'But then why did he say nice things about Hera?'

'To show how upset he is,' Hermes said promptly. 'He's telling you that she's not the problem – you are.'

'W-WHY?'

'Think about it for a sec. Hercules once banished you because you put Zoe in danger. And now you've only gone and done it again, right?'

Tim felt more tears prickle at his eyes. He nodded.

Hermes placed a firm hand on Tim's shoulder. 'After all, you keep provoking Hera.

Hercules probably thinks that if you stayed away, Zoe would be safe.'

'Gah! I'll have to apologise!' Tim cried. 'I don't want them to hate me.' He slid himself off the wall, but Hermes grasped his shoulder to stop him dashing off.

'I'd leave it for now if I were you,' the god said. 'Give 'em a chance to cool off a bit. Let 'em get over it.'

Tim didn't want to wait. He wanted to sort things out straight away.

'You'll only make it worse,' Hermes warned, not loosening his grip. 'Look, how about this. Let Hercules cool down, and then I'll go talk to him myself. Tell him he's being a jerk and to get over it. But not right now. Can you do that, Tim

Baker? Can you wait, for the sake of your friendship?' The god looked deep into Tim's eyes.

Tim found himself nodding. 'I guess.'

Hermes exhaled. 'Good. Smart kid.' He patted Tim's shoulder.

'So I may as well go home—' Tim started to say.

'Not necessarily.' Hermes slid off the wall and stood next to Tim. 'Actually, I was wondering. Seeing as you're here, could you do me a favour?'

HOPELESS HEROES

To download Hopeless Heroes

ACTIVITIES
AND
POSTERS

visit:
www.sweetcherrypublishing.com/resources

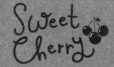